FOUR WINDS PRESS ❖ *New York*

MAXWELL MACMILLAN CANADA   *Toronto*   MAXWELL MACMILLAN INTERNATIONAL *New York*   *Oxford*   *Singapore*   *Sydney*

In Dolphin Time

by DIANE FARRIS

Acknowledgments

There has been a loving circle of friends, family, and colleagues who have walked
with me on this dolphin journey, which has spanned more than a decade: Vera
and Bill Farris, my parents, Hope and Tony White, Mary Taylor, Deborah Harris,
Mary Fox, Penny Boyes-Braem, Marilyn Asse, Jerry Uelsmann, Mary Shaw May,
Lola Haskins, John Cech, and Virginia Duncan, my editor. My son, Andrew
Uelsmann, has grown up with these dolphins and helps me see them in new light.
Ted Runions, my husband, has given me his sustaining belief and presence.

Copyright © 1994 by F. Diane Farris   All rights reserved. No part of this book may be reproduced
or transmitted in any form or by any means, electronic or mechanical, including photocopying,
recording, or by any information storage and retrieval system, without permission in writing from
the Publisher. Four Winds Press, Macmillan Publishing Company, 866 Third Avenue, New York,
NY 10022. Maxwell Macmillan Canada, Inc., 1200 Eglinton Avenue East, Suite 200, Don Mills,
Ontario M3C 3N1. Macmillan Publishing Company is part of the Maxwell Communication
Group of Companies. First edition. Printed in the United States of America on recycled paper.
10 9 8 7 6 5 4 3 2 1   The text of this book is set in Garamond No. 3. Book design
by Christy Hale. Library of Congress Cataloging-in-Publication Data   Farris, Diane. In dolphin
time / by Diane Farris.— 1st ed.   p.   cm.   Summary: A child carries two dolphins home from
the beach in a pocket, keeps them in the bathtub for a while, and finds that they make the ordinary
wonderful and the wonderful ordinary.   ISBN 0-02-734365-0   [1. Dolphins—Fiction.] I. Title.
PZ7.F24619In 1994 [E]—dc20 92-42512

For Ted and Andrew

The light gathers.

A dolphin rises.
Then another.
They are curious,
and as kind as the ocean is deep.

A few days ago, I remembered
that I had forgotten
something in my pocket ... dolphins.

I don't know how they came to
be there or when...could dolphins
always be so close by?
    They were light in my hand,
and dry to the touch. When I eased them
gently into a bowl, they looked content...
but crowded.

I moved them to the bath,
dolphins smiling in the tub.
The day you discover dolphins in your pocket
is a day of wonder...a day of delight.

I began noticing dolphins everywhere.

Often,
and in unexpected
places.

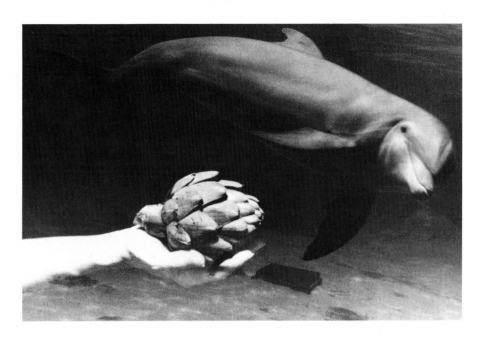

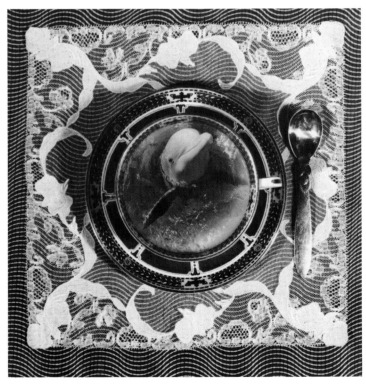

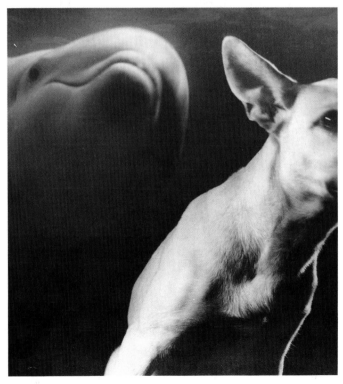

They made the ordinary wonderful
and the wonderful ordinary.

I was enchanted by
their way of speaking,
but wondered if they made up some
of the stories they told,

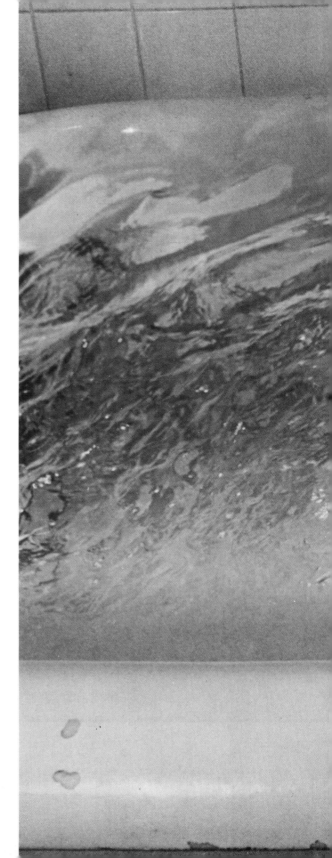

of cloud-dancing...
swimming free...
of coming close...
and wishing on an underwater moon.

After many smiling dolphin days,
they let me know they must return
to the ocean, their own deep home.

At the shore, the water was alive
with light that began with us
and never ended.

They shared one more dolphin secret,
that friends are always near.
They would return, and very soon.
Remember, they smiled.

Look gently. Anticipate surprise.